AF431126

To Jack,

Go fast. Be Yourself. Love yourself.

I love you!

When I go, I go fast.

I'm the fastest kid to ever go.

Going fast is what I do.

I do good things,
I'll share a few.

I do the dishes.

I clean the floors.

I'm always first
to open doors.

I do all my chores
without delay.

So I have more time
to go and play.

When I play I play
with all my might.

Sometimes I play
until its night.

When nighttime comes,

I need to slow down.

I cross my legs
and sit on the ground.

I take some deep breaths,

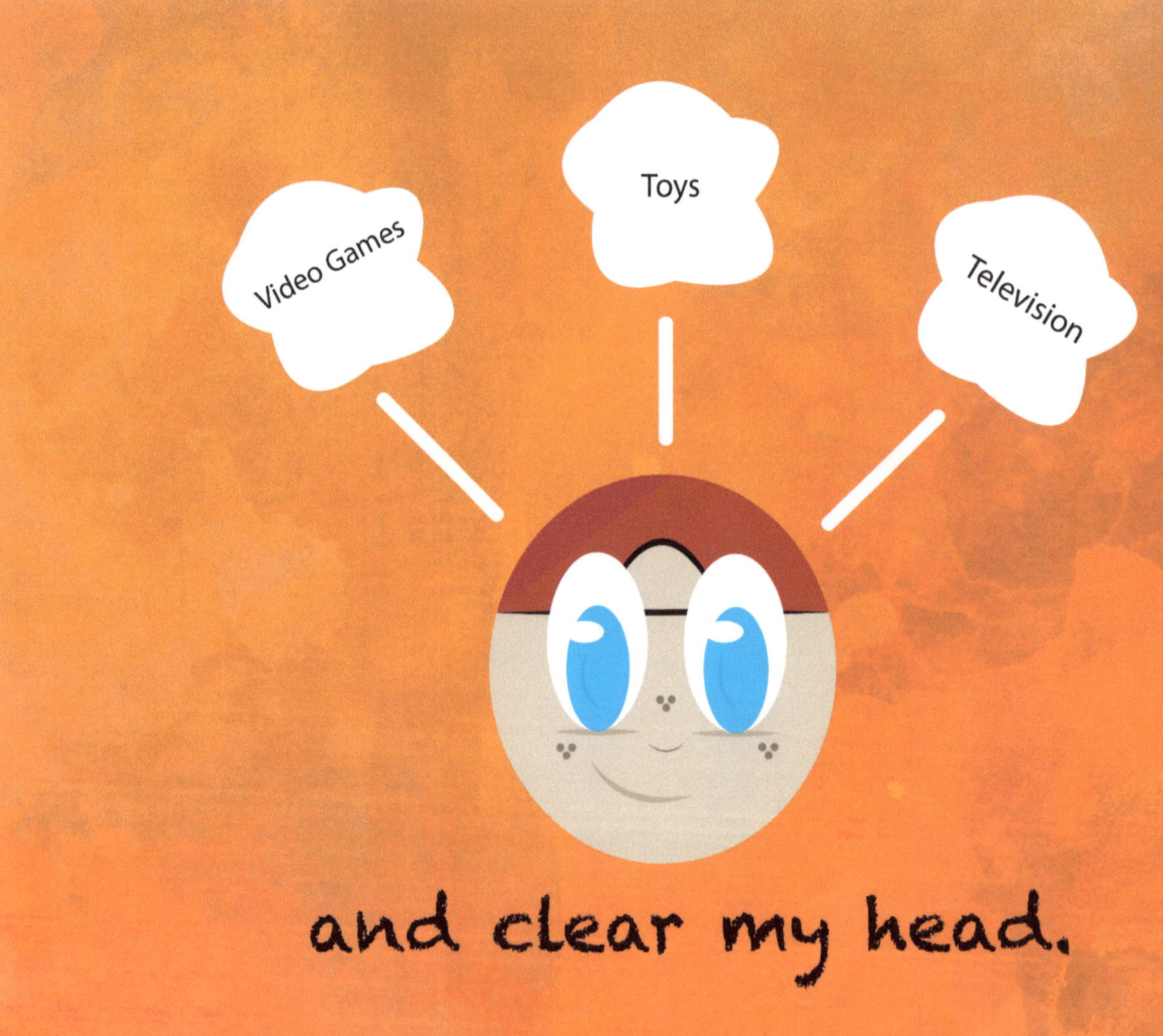


and clear my head.

I put on my PJs
and hop in the bed.

I say my prayers,

and grab a sip of a drink.

So thats my day,
What do you think?

If you use your energy
to help do good.

You'll feel better and
act as you should.

doing good things
can be a blast.

Always Help.

Always be polite.

And always remember,

That you are your parents light.

The End